Tenpin penguins

Russell Punter

Illustrated by David Semple

At the penguins' bowling alley
there's a contest on today.

1st Prize

Benji   0
Gwyneth 0
Penny   0

The winner gets a crate of fish.
They just can't wait to play.

Whoever knocks down fifty pins
takes home the splendid prize.

Benji's first to bowl a ball.
"Just watch this shot!" he cries.

Benji   0
Gwyneth   0
Penny   0

The ball goes rolling down a slope
and grows a coat of snow.

He doesn't hit a single pin.

I've gone wrong, like before.

Next time, Benji tries too hard.
His ball flies through the air.

His fourth ball zooms off skyward too
and lands up who knows where?

Benji   0
Gwynneth   21
Penny   30

Benji has one final try.
But thanks to icy snow...

"Wooooah!" moans Benji, in a daze.

Benji	0
Gwyneth	28
Penny	40

He spins head over tail.

At least he strikes a pin this time,
as out of sight it sails.

Penny Penguin takes the prize —
she knocked down every pin.

Poor Benji only managed one.
He's sad he didn't win.

But as the penguins waddle home,
there comes an odd surprise...

A snowman with a red pin nose,
and bowling balls for eyes!

"Did you make this?" Sea Lion asks.

South Pole Snowman Contest

"I guess so," Benji sighs.

It's the South Pole Snowman Contest, son.

And you've just won first prize!

About phonics

Phonics is a method of teaching reading which is used extensively in today's schools. At its heart is an emphasis on identifying the *sounds* of letters, or combinations of letters, that are then put together to make words. These sounds are known as phonemes.

Starting to read

Learning to read is an important milestone for any child. The process can begin well before children start to learn letters and put them together to read words. The sooner children can discover books and enjoy stories and language, the better they will be prepared for reading themselves, first with the help of an adult and then independently.

You can find out more about phonics on the Usborne website at **usborne.com/Phonics**

Phonemic awareness

An important early stage in pre-reading and early reading is developing phonemic awareness: that is, listening out for the sounds within words. Rhymes, rhyming stories and alliteration are excellent ways of encouraging phonemic awareness.

In this story, your child will soon identify the *e* sound, as in **penguins.** Look out, too, for rhymes such as **no – snow** and **pin – win.**

Hearing your child read

If your child is reading a story to you, don't rush to correct mistakes, but be ready to prompt or guide if he or she is struggling. Above all, do give plenty of praise and encouragement.

Edited by Lesley Sims
Designed by Hope Reynolds

Reading consultants: Alison Kelly and Anne Washtell

First published in 2021 by Usborne Publishing Ltd., Usborne House, 83-85 Saffron Hill,
London EC1N 8RT, England. usborne.com Copyright © 2021 Usborne Publishing Ltd.

First published in America in 2021. UE. EDC, Tulsa, Oklahoma 74146. usbornebooksandmore.com
Library of Congress Control Number: 2021935920